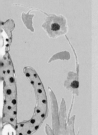

E FICTION HOL

Holt, Sharon.

Did my mother do that?

10/13

For my mum, Margaret. Thanks for what you did.
S. H.

For my mother, Isobel
B. L.

Text copyright © 2009 by Sharon Holt
Illustrations copyright © 2009 by Brian Lovelock

First U.S. edition 2010

Library of Congress Cataloging-in-Publication Data

Holt, Sharon.
Did my mother do that? / Sharon Holt ; illustrated by Brian Lovelock. —1st U.S. ed.
p. cm.
Summary: With the promise of hearing about the day she was born, Holly and her father
first imagine the birth of several different animals including chickens, kittens, and kangaroos.
ISBN 978-0-7636-4685-1
[1. Animals—Infancy—Fiction. 2. Birth—Fiction. 3. Childbirth—Fiction.]
I. Lovelock, Brian, ill. II. Title.
PZ7.H74158Di 2010
[E]—dc22   2009033083

10 11 12 13 14 15 CCP 10 9 8 7 6 5 4 3 2 1

Printed in Shenzhen, Guangdong, China

This book was typeset in Village.
The illustrations were done in watercolor, acrylic ink, and colored pencil.

Candlewick Press
99 Dover Street
Somerville, Massachusetts 02144

visit us at www.candlewick.com

Did My Mother Do That?

SHARON HOLT

illustrated by BRIAN LOVELOCK

CANDLEWICK PRESS

Holly didn't want Mommy to go out.

"Daddy will tell you a story,"
said Mommy.

"Yes," said Daddy. "I'll tell you a story
about when you were a new baby."

"Okay," said Holly.
"Did I hatch out of an egg like
 a chicken when I was new?"

"No," said Daddy. "If you were a
new chick, your mother would
have fluffed up her feathers and
sat on you to keep you safe.
Your mother didn't do that."

Holly laughed and asked,
"What if I were a kitten?"

"If you were a kitten, your mother
would have licked you all over,"
said Daddy. "Your mother didn't do that."

Holly giggled as Daddy
licked the air with
his tongue.

"What if I were
a baby kangaroo?"

"If you were a baby kangaroo, Mommy would have kept you in her pocket," said Daddy. He looked in his pocket and shook his head. "Your mother didn't do that."

"What if I were a baby owl?" asked Holly.

"If you were a baby owl, your mother would have fed you mice," said Daddy. "Your mother didn't do that."

Holly and Daddy scrunched up their faces at the thought of eating mice.

"What if I were a baby shark?"

"You don't want to hear about baby sharks," said Daddy.

"Yes, I do," said Holly. "What would my mother do if I were a baby shark?"

"Well," said Daddy. "When a
mother shark gives birth, she has
so many baby sharks that she
eats some of them for dinner!"

Holly hid under the blankets.

"Don't worry," said Daddy.
"Your mother would never do that."

"Good," said Holly.
"I'm glad my mother isn't a shark.
What if I were a baby sea horse?"

"If you were a baby sea horse,
your father would have looked
after you in his belly," said Daddy.

"Really?" asked Holly. "Did you
look after me in your belly?"

"No," said Daddy. "Your mother carried you in her belly. Mommy looked after you, and I looked after Mommy."

"So what *did* Mommy do when I was a new baby?" asked Holly.

"When you were a new baby, your mother held you close to her heart and cried," said Daddy.

Holly looked worried.
"Was she very sad?" she asked.

"No," said Daddy, tucking Holly in to bed. "They were happy tears. When you were born, your mother was the happiest mommy in the world. And I was the happiest daddy in the world."

Holly smiled.

"And I was the happiest
baby in the world."

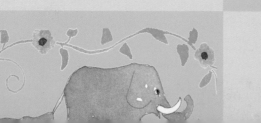